The
First Fairy Tale

Book II: *The Awakening Heart*

Written by Susan Highsmith
Illustrated by Mark Sean Wilson

Words Matter Publishing
P.O. Box 531
Salem, Il 62881
www.wordsmatterpublishing.com

IISBN 13: 978-1-947072-75-6
ISBN 10: 1-947072-75-7

Library of Congress Catalog Card Number: 2018945486

The
First Fairy Tale

Book II: *The Awakening Heart*

Written by Susan Highsmith
Illustrated by Mark Sean Wilson

Dedication

*For all of us who have taken this journey ~
for all those precious ones yet to come . . .*

The First Fairy Tale Book II: The Awakening Heart

Dear Reader:

The story you are about to read describes a journey we have all taken. It resumes the travels described in *The First Fairy Tale Book I: The Adventure Begins*. The stories are allegories that remind us of the process we underwent to develop the magnificent human bodies we wear throughout our time here on Earth.

These stories are not new. They have been told and retold throughout the generations as fairy tales, fables, myths, legends, folklore, parables and spiritual metaphors urging us to recognize our exquisite beginnings and appreciate the perils that we faced—and overcame—along the way. Children resonate with these stories. They delight in hearing how the travelers overcome obstacles and succeed in building a new home. On deep inner levels, they know the story portrays their own journeys in a warm, entertaining manner. *The First Fairy Tale* trilogy recounts an ideal passage; thus each story promotes healing if a child's personal journey into embodiment was less than ideal.

The ability of a fertilized egg to develop in the manner and time that it does is wondrous indeed. The story of conception itself is told in *The First Fairy Tale Book I,* while *Fairy Tale II* continues the journey, describing the first three weeks of gestation. As the journeys of egg and sperm were hazardous, so is the next phase of the journey traversed by the beautiful new Being evolving from the union of these two energies. Life is growing at such an accelerated pace! This essential part of development is to be especially treasured and celebrated.

This story, like *The First Fairy Tale: Book I*, embodies the essence of Prenatal and Perinatal Psychology. It symbolically describes the embryology of the first few weeks after conception which includes implantation, the formation of the heart, and concludes as the heart begins to beat. Again, a more scientific explanation of this magnificent process in included in the epilogue following the fairy tale. As I said before, the tale is really enough. We truly know it by heart.

Not just once but many times,
and not just long ago but even now, new life begins.
It grows with such speed that even Mother Nature is in awe.

1

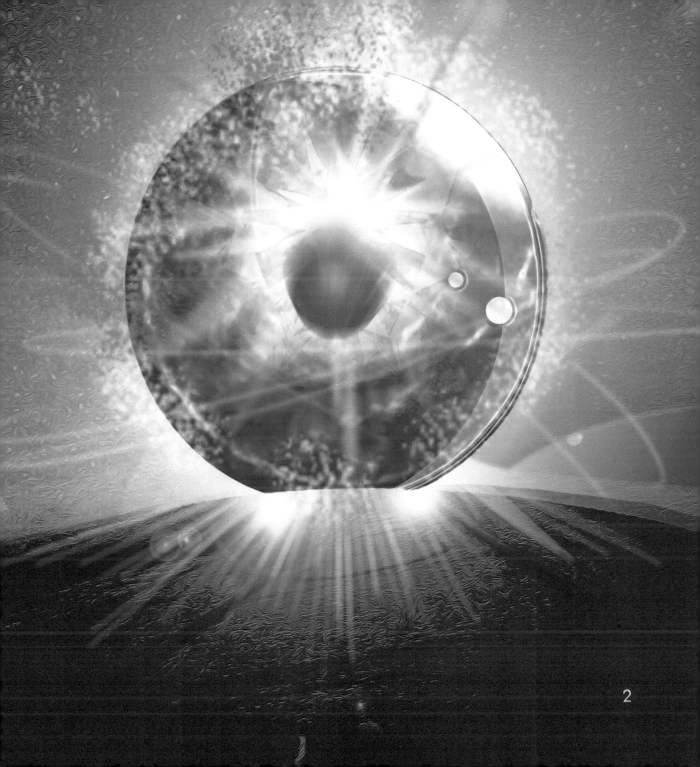

Infinite Spirit,
All Knowing,
looks upon Mother Earth
and sees there is an opportunity to learn,
grow, and expand the Consciousness of All That Is.

4

In a Union of male and female
taking place on Planet Earth,
two have come together
and a temple is being created
to house a unique expression of the Divine.

Units multiply –
One becomes two,
two become four,
four become eight,
eight become sixteen,
sixteen become thirty-two,
thirty-two become sixty-four,
sixty-four become one hundred twenty eight . . .
and on it goes.
Each Little One knows exactly what it is to do.

8

As each unit divides and multiplies,
it remains in contact with the others.
They are a team, growing into a Being that will
contain them all, as this tiny bundle does now.

10

This time, as it has before,
the Essence of an Eternal Spirit
will reside in a Body Temple of its choosing.
This will allow the Spirit to navigate on Planet Earth.
It will move and breathe and have a will of its own.
Yet, the temple will always have within it –
the Guiding Spirit.

On the Earth, within a Chalice, it travels.
It moves through a narrow corridor – to where?

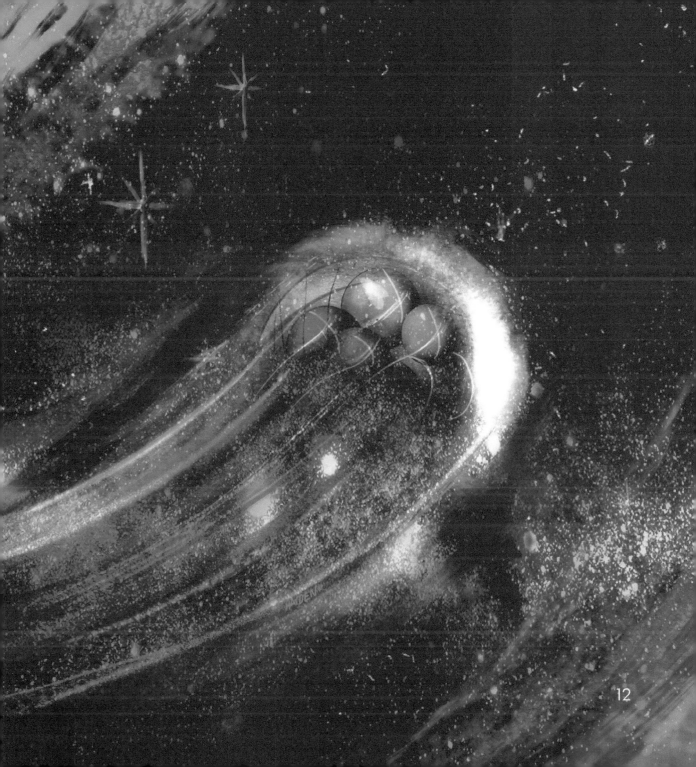

12

The Little Ones ask each other,

"Where are we going?

Will the journey be long?

Are we there yet?"

 The tiny vessel moves slowly, cautiously.

It revolves in liquid light that propels it further onward.

Suddenly the sphere tumbles and turns.

It is falling.

Over the precipice it plunges,

downward into the abyss.

Where are they?
The ensemble trembles as they float,
blindly seeking a place to land.

Will this be their home?
Will the landscape be inviting?

18

The little temple-builders are united in their objective.
They must find a place to land and establish their colony.
They must find a receptive location to berth
or they will perish!

20

The sphere bumps into a soft, inviting surface.

This environment seems like a good place to land.

They could burrow in here.

But The first attempt to land fails!

They must find the perfect landing site

and allow it to welcome them.

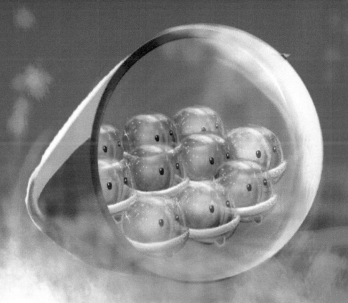

The travelers bring gifts from afar,
and will receive gifts from this foreign land.
The craft nestles into this welcoming place.
It feels like Home –
at least for now.

The environment seems to reach out
and embrace the little group of travelers.
Here, there is the promise of nourishment,
and a relationship that will cultivate its growth.

Indeed, the lush garden in which the temple will be built
is designed to receive the Spirit,
and will nurture the growth of its precious residents.

In the silence of this warm and hospitable terrain,
the voyagers rest.
In this moment of comfort, tenderly held,
the band of travelers realize that,
in this secure site, they will express their uniqueness, and
they will truly unite,
blending each of their qualities
to create a single and entirely new identity.

Their growth continues,
now rapid and compelling.
Expanding in rhythm with the Universe,
each critical phase is carried out with precision,
and with awareness of the Love that guides it.

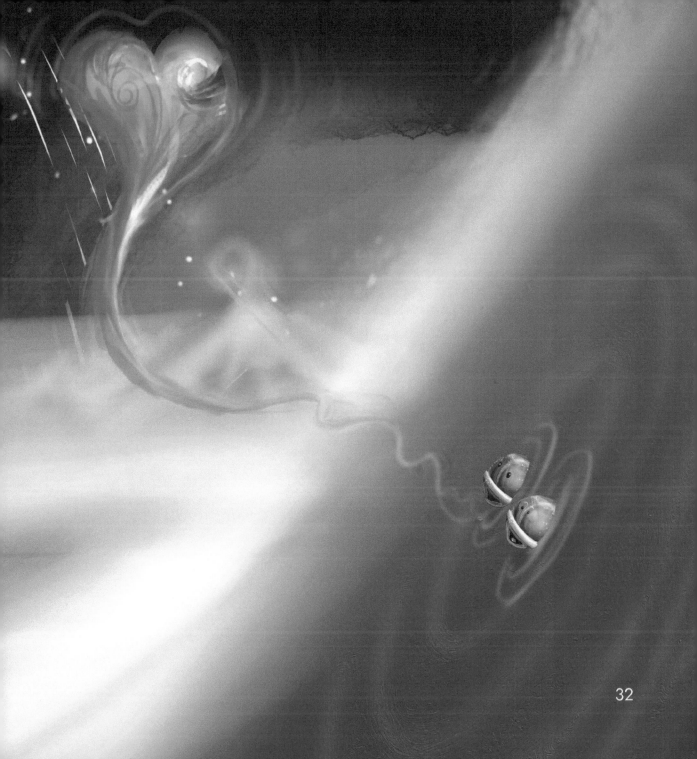

Anticipation mounts.

Something miraculous is about to occur.

Individuals cooperate,

as if in response to Divine orchestration.

34

Some of the Temple Builders are guided to form a magnificent structure that resembles a Symbol of Infinity.

 Others nestle against this contour
assembling into a rosy red chamber.

Each Little One knows its role,
and gravitates to the perfect location,
becoming a part of the ideal configuration
that will serve in harmony with the others.

38

Now, working in unison,
chamber music sounds.

The Heart begins to pulse.
This rhythm will last a lifetime.

On the twenty-second day,
of this incredible journey,
this Heart begins to beat.

40

The music – the energy and vibration of the Universe –
surges through this Divine Instrument.

A Heart! The seat of Love has taken form in this new Being.

Within this heart, a spark ignites.
Plumes of sapphire blue,
crystalline pink, and sunshine yellow,
lie hidden within it –
promising another awakening.

42

In the wisdom of this Newness,
a grander Knowing holds the vision of
expansion beyond this small beating heart.

Life is readying for more –
more what, this eager Heart wonders?
There is a mission to accomplish.

Love IS the mission!
To BE LOVE on Earth!
This time the Heart will be honored.
It will remember its Divine Mission.

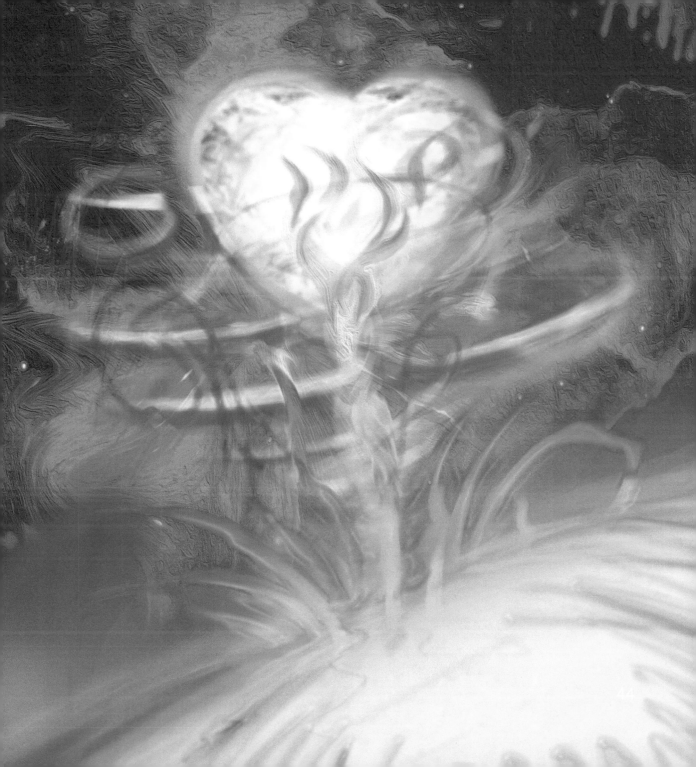

What will it become? the Heart wonders,
dreaming of a day when all will be ready
to leave the warm, wet, darkness
and emerge into Light –
a Light it has always known.

This time the Heart will succeed.
Radiating Power, Wisdom, and Love, it cannot fail.

Epilogue

For Parents' Eyes Only

If you are reading this story to your Little One, please know that this epilogue is not for your child's ears. This explanation is meant to help you, as a parent appreciate the embryology that occurs so early and so rapidly in the womb. Your child understands on a deep level the meaning of the fairy tale, which is a metaphor for the miraculous journey undertaken to come into a human body. Little Ones just need to hear how cherished they are, and have their miraculous passages acknowledged.

Babies do not tire of hearing the story of an idealic journey into life while being held in your arms and being told they are loved beyond measure. These words and actions build the foundations of self esteem that children require to reach their full potential. They can appreciate this story even if it is read to them while they are still in the womb.

From the moment of conception, the new Being created by the merging of egg and sperm grows exponentially. In the first three weeks of development the baby's physical heart forms and begins to beat. It is cradled in the embrace of the neural tube, the primitive cells and tissues that evolve into the brain and nervous system.

n the first week the conceptus travels down the mother's fallopian tube, cells dividing and multiplying as they drift to the intersection with the uterus itself. The cluster of growing cells changes names according to science: it is first known as a zygote (which means joined together), then a morula (named for the Latin term for mulberry), then a blastocyst (from two Greek terms that mean sprout and capsule). Within ten days it falls into the vastness of the womb where, if all goes well, it will implant in the lining of mother's uterus. Mother Nature is an extraordinary tender of her creations, so if all is not well, the imperfect cells will pass from the mother's body during her next menstrual cycle.

Implantation is the major task during week two. In this process the blastocyst embeds in the inner wall of the uterus and begins to receive nourishment from Mother. Stem cells, the building blocks from which all bodily structures develop, are present. These cells are capable of differentiating, that is, becoming specialized to suit the requirements of the growing embryo. As implantation is occurring, the placenta and umbilical cord are forming.

By week three, three layers of tissue have formed (inner/endoderm, middle/mesoderm, and outer/ectoderm), and will further differentiate into specific structures with specific functions. A rudimentary circulation system has come on line and by day 22, baby's precious heart begins to beat!

Acknowledge and celebrate your baby's (and your own) magnificent accomplishment by reading this tale aloud, while your child is still in utero or after your baby is born. Babies love this story and your bond will grow as you let your Little One know that you recognize what a wonder-full job is being accomplished in the sacred space of Mother's womb—or has been accomplished now that you can look into each others' eyes.